This book is dedicated to all children who dream with fun and creative imaginations. May they work hard and help others by growing up spreading beauty, hope, and friendship throughout the world.

A special thank you to Charlene Torkelson for her help with the editing of this book.

> ***The Fairy Code***
> *"Spread beauty, hope, and friendship by working hard and helping others."*

BLOSSOM LAND

AND

THE MAGICAL WISHING

WELL

BY

PATTY RONCHETTO

This book was printed in the United States of America.
Copyright © 2014 Patty Ronchetto

ISBN-13: 978-1500362485

ISBN-10: 1500362484

TABLE OF CONTENTS

BLOSSOM LAND
AND
THE MAGICAL WISHING WELL

Prologue

The Invitation

"Graduation Ceremonies will be held at the Magic Wishing Well in Blossom Land's Fairy Garden just before sunset on December 31. Students who have successfully completed their missions and lived by the code of the fairies, will be rewarded with a treasure chest. The treasure chest will reveal your gift of magical power. A joyous celebration will follow."

----Signed Professor DoGood

Professor DoGood, the teacher of Blossom Land's Fairy School, sat at his desk feeling a little sad while addressing invitations for this year's graduation.

Fairies go to school all year long with no summer vacation. It was now September, and he would be handing out the invitations early, hoping to encourage students who were not doing their best to work harder. Professor DoGood did not want any of his students to miss the joyous and magical graduation celebration. He was getting on in years but still wanted to keep teaching. He had just come from a meeting with Miss Cinnamon. Miss Cinnamon was the Principal of Blossom Land Fairy School. Together, Professor DoGood and Miss Cinnamon decided those students who had successfully followed the fairy code to "Spread beauty, hope, and friendship by working hard and helping others." Once each student had been passed onto graduation, their magical gifts would be revealed.

In the meeting, Miss Cinnamon and Professor DoGood went through each student's record. They were happy that most students would have no problem graduating. There were a few students who needed to be spoken to about spending too much time playing and not enough time working in their gardens, or they lacked attention in class.

Miss Cinnamon had some exciting news! She would be getting married early next year to Mr. Frost, who was also a school teacher. He lived across town and taught at another school. Professor DoGood was happy for the young couple but also saddened that Miss Cinnamon would be leaving Blossom Land Fairy School.

Miss Cinnamon's replacement, Mr. Snarley, was also at the meeting. He came from Woodland Patch, another fairy village not far from Blossom Land. It is a wooded land without much color as it is mostly shade with all the trees. Flowers do not grow well without sunshine. Mr. Snarley does not understand why Blossom Land fairies spend so much time working to grow beautiful flowers in their fairy gardens. He will be making changes for next year.

Like people, fairies are all different in size, shape, and color, except they never get taller than four inches and that is a tall fairy! Professor DoGood is only three inches tall and quite heavy around the middle (he loves his chocolate pixie treats). His eyesight is not what it used to be. He now wears thick, round glasses and must admit that his lack of hair on top of his head makes him look older than his 102 years. He always wears a black square college cap on his bald head. His black flowing robe helps to cover his oversized middle. Fairies can live to be very old compared to humans. They graduate from school at the age of ten. Really good fairies may live to be 150 years old if they spend their lifetimes growing beautiful flowers and helping others by using their magical powers.

Mr. Snarley is a tall, thin fairy. He tops out at the full four inches. He does not have a sweet tooth so that is probably why he is so skinny. He has a big, black mustache that curls up on each end. He believes that fairies of Blossom Land spend too much time in their gardens and dress too colorfully. His mission is to change the way of teaching the student fairies. These are his requests:

1.   Cut the fairy gardens in half so the land can be used to build fairy condos.

2.   Fairy school students must graduate by the age of eight, not ten.

3.   Charge money for all the flowers grown in the fairy gardens. Blossom Land fairies deliver flowers at no cost to anyone, humans or fairies. Flowers are given to those in the hospital or home sick to cheer them up. Mr. Snarley wants to charge money for any flowers sent. He also wants to set up flower stands to sell the flowers. This would help pay for the condos.

4. Fairies are to wear navy blue and white school uniforms so all fairies look alike.

Fairies in Mr. Snarley's Woodland Patch live in the hollows of trees but the Blossom Land fairies live in gardens, by ponds, or under little mushroom caps. Some even share a nest with the birds. Fairies can live in the trees if the weather gets too cold or snowy, but they love to be surrounded by fragrant, colorful flowers.

In Blossom Land time is spent teaching the fairies how to nurture their gardens and live by the fairy code of "Spread beauty, hope, and friendship by working hard and helping others." These are important things to learn, and it takes time.

Fairies do not need money. Their goal in life is what the fairy code states. Mr. Snarley thinks it is important to modernize Blossom Land and start running it as a business like humans do. Fairies are different from humans. They are very shy so you won't see them often. They hide outside in gardens because they love the fresh air, sunshine, and all the different smells and colors of the flowers. They have little wings that help them fly around. They flutter very fast like hummingbirds. The fairies in Blossom Land grow the flowers that represent the month they were born. They enjoy dressing up in the colorful flowers they grow and wearing their birthstone jewels. Mr. Snarley wants to change all that. He wants all the fairies to dress alike. He even told Miss Cinnamon he would like to get a little car to drive around Blossom Land. Fairies can fly and don't have any automobiles in the gardens as they do not want to pollute the air.

Can you imagine how unhappy the fairies will be with these new rules? And what will become of Professor DoGood?

Chapter One

Snowdrop

It is the middle of September, and Snowdrop is so excited to have received her invitation for the upcoming graduation! She is a good student and has done well to learn all her gardening skills but each day she wants to play with her friends before her work in the garden is done. Snowdrop was born on the second day of January. She has dark hair and eyes. She was named Snowdrop because there were many little drops of snow on the pink flowers the day she was born. Those flowers are called **carnations**, and they are the flower for January. The **carnation** has many colors and have meanings of affection, love, and true friendship. Snowdrop loves to wear **carnations** in her hair. She likes all colors but her favorite is pink and red. She wears a red **garnet** birthstone necklace.

On this day, Snowdrop runs excitedly up to her parents to show them the invitation.

"Mother, Father, look what I received today! I am so excited. I know that I will graduate with all my friends this year. I want to wear the prettiest pink flower dress."

"This is wonderful, Snowdrop," her mother replies. "Just be sure that you continue with your studies. You need to keep your grades up through the end of the school year."

Snowdrop's father smiles and hugs his little girl but then gets serious. He does not want Snowdrop to be disappointed. He gives her some advice, "Snowdrop, to be sure you won't have any problems before graduation, I want you to promise me that you will tend to your garden first before playing and visiting with your friends. You were born in January. As you know, fairies born in January are known to be very good friends, but you must put your studying first and your best friends will understand. Simply tell them you can't play until your studies are done."

"OK, Father, I promise," Snowdrop responds. "One thing I don't understand is that I am a good student, so why do I have to wait to find out until the day of graduation if I have made it? It seems silly to me, don't you think?"

"Snowdrop," her mother replies, "we are different from humans. Humans graduate after successfully learning all their studies, and then they go to work. Fairies have a special calling, a different kind of work. We need to always be helpful and caring to others. There are always lessons to be learned. December 31, on your tenth year, is that special day that you learn the most valuable lesson of all. Be patient and practice the fairy code every day."

"Mother, what magical gift do you think I will receive?" Snowdrop asks.

"Just continue living the fairy code, be happy, and on December 31, you will know." Snowdrop still did not understand. She decided to go and talk to her friend, Freddy. Maybe he could help her understand and be more patient until the end of the year.

Chapter Two

Freddy the Flirt

February is the shortest month of the year, but it can be a very busy month in Blossom Land. That is because there are Presidents' birthdays and Valentine's Day. Valentine's Day is February 14, and fairies like to send secret messages to their favorite Valentine. They must do this when they are not tending to their gardens.

Freddy was born in February. He likes to fly after and throw kisses to the girl fairies. Everyone says he acts this way because he was born on Valentine's Day and thinks all the girls are his sweethearts. His nickname is Freddy the Flirt. The girl fairies think he is cute, but the boy fairies say he is just plain silly! He likes to tell stories and talks a lot in fairy school, but he is smart and quick to give the correct answers when the fairy teacher, Professor DoGood, calls on him.

Freddy says his favorite color is red like the Valentine heart. He secretly likes Snowdrop the best out of all the girl fairies, and he knows that her favorite color is also red.

The flower for February is a **violet.** It is purple in color. Sometimes Freddy looks too colorful because he wears bright red with purple! His parents had given him an **amethyst** ring for his birthday. **Amethyst** is his birthstone, and it is purple. Maybe someday he will give the ring to Snowdrop!

February only has 28 days except every four years an extra day is added to make February have 29 days. Freddy is very happy that he wasn't born on February 29. He would not like celebrating his birthday only every four years! Freddy asked Professor DoGood why every four years an extra day is added in February. It may be difficult to understand but this is what the professor told him:

"The time it takes the earth to orbit the sun once is a year. Twelve months make a year. Scientists have discovered that it isn't that simple because it takes the earth a little longer to complete going around (orbiting) the sun. It takes 365 days, 5 hours, 48 minutes and 46 seconds (about 365 ¼ days). Those extra hours will add up so that after four years the calendar would be out of step by one day. Adding one day every four years catches up so that the twelve month calendar will match the orbit of the sun."

Whew! That is a difficult one to understand.

Freddy was reading over his invitation when Snowdrop arrived. They sat down together under a big mushroom cap.

"Freddy, what do you think our gift of magical powers will be?" Snowdrop asked.

"I only hope I will find out," Freddy replied.

"Oh Freddy," Snowdrop laughed. "You really are silly. All the fairies know how smart you are and so does Professor DoGood. Why do you think that you won't have your magical power revealed on graduation day?"

Freddy hung his head and said, "Well, I noticed that when Professor DoGood handed me my graduation invitation, he did not look happy. I hope it wasn't because there may be a problem with me graduating. Maybe I need to stop being so silly."

"I am worried too, Freddy," Snowdrop admitted. "I spend too much time visiting with my friends before getting my work done. My mom and dad told me to finish all my work before I play with my friends. I think I should explain to my friends this is something I must do and hope they will understand."

"Maybe I should try to not be so silly. I am going to be on my best behavior, and I should tell my friends too, so they won't think I am mad at them." Freddy said.

"I know, Freddy, let's get all of our friends who are graduating this year together and explain to them. Let's tell them during lunch at fairy school tomorrow, and then we will meet at the Magic Wishing Well after school."

Chapter Three

The Graduation Class

It was agreed then that Snowdrop and Freddy would pass the word along to meet after school at the Magic Wishing Well. They would need to let their classmates know.

There was Patrick, born March 17, St. Patrick's Day. Patrick liked to dress in green because St. Patrick's Day represents his Irish heritage. He has planted little four leaf clovers in the fairy garden but also must grow **daffodils** as that is his birth month flower. **Daffodils** are yellow, and Patrick sometimes wears them upside down on his head like a hat. He is a little guy and likes to tell jokes to all the other fairies. Like Freddy, he sometimes jokes around too much. For his last birthday, Patrick's parents gave him a new belt with a beautiful light blue stone on the belt buckle. The stone is **aquamarine**. Aqua means water and marine means sea. This stone is known for protecting sailors for a safe voyage on the ocean. Its magical meaning is "to calm" so Patrick's parents thought it was a good one to help calm down his joke telling.

The smallest of fairies living in Blossom Land is named Sweet Pea. Born in April, she is named after her monthly flower, **sweet pea.** The **sweet pea** flower is a climbing flower and comes in a variety of colors. Sweet Pea likes to wrap many colors of the climbing flowers around her head like a crown. She likes the deep pink flower the best but enjoys being one of the most colorful fairies, so she sometimes wears all the colors of her flower on her dress and in her hair. Sweet Pea's parents did something a little different for her birthday this year. The jewel for April is **diamond**. It is clear in color and sparkles. Sweet Pea's parents decided to give her little clusters of diamonds, kind of like glitter. Using the diamond glitter, Sweet Pea adds it to her flower crown and sprinkles and glues it on her dress with the different flower colors. She is truly a "sparkling" fairy. The magical meaning of the **diamond** is love, and Sweet Pea is truly filled with the spirit of love. Everyone adores Sweet Pea because she is so sweet! She never says a bad word about anyone, even if she doesn't agree with them. She believes that everyone has their own opinion.

Snowdrop asked her friend, Lily, to help spread the word. Lily is very good at planning get-togethers. She plans the big Springtime Maypole Celebration. Lily was born in May, one of the most beautiful months in Blossom Land. On the first day of May, all the fairies gather and build a "maypole" to celebrate springtime. A maypole is a tall pole decorated with colorful ribbons and flowers. The center pole is decorated with garlands of flowers and the different colored ribbons are attached to a spinning disc on top of the pole. Each fairy grabs a hanging ribbon and when the music begins they dance and spin around ducking under each other and wrapping the ribbons around the maypole. The fairies do this maypole dance to welcome spring, and it begins the May Day sporting events and dances. It is a very festive day with both the boy and girl fairies participating in the events. They also paint their birth month flowers on their faces. Like Sweet Pea, Lily is named after her birth month flower. The flower for May is **lily of the valley.** Lily wears her birthstone jewel, beautiful green **emerald** earrings every day to match her deep green eyes.

The meaning of the **emerald** is good fortune and youth. It is a symbol of rebirth like spring is the rebirth of the seasons.

Lily was happy to help with rounding up the rest of the classmates. There were two sets of twins in the class this year. Alex and Alyssa, brother and sister, were born June 10. Alex was the first to be born. A few minutes later his sister, Alyssa was born.

It just so happens that June is a month that has two flowers and two jewels. Alex was named after the jewel **alexandrite**. It is also known as the **"moonstone."** Its meaning is for good health and a long life. The stone itself is a strong gem with colors changing like a chameleon. The color can appear as a lovely green in daylight and then turn to a purplish red at night. Alex wears his stone on his wrist like a watch. His parents chose the flower **honeysuckle** for him. This was a good choice because the **honeysuckle** flower is mostly white in color, and as his birthstone can change colors, the white flower will blend in with any color. Alex loves to feed the hummingbirds by growing many **honeysuckle** flowers. The flowers have a sweet nectar food in them that the hummingbirds suck out with their long beaks.

Alex's sister, Alyssa, was given the **pearl** as her special stone. **Pearls** come from living sea creatures called oysters. Like Alex's jewel, the **pearl** also has reference to the moon. There is an old saying that the **pearl** was born when a single drop of rain fell from the heavens and became the "heart" of the oyster. Some people believe **pearls** are teardrops of the moon that are formed by passage of angels through the clouds of heaven. The meaning of the **pearl** is honesty and wisdom. **Pearls** can be different colors but are usually white or ivory. Alyssa made her **pearl** into a pin and wears in on her dress, close to her heart. Alyssa's parents decided to give her the **rose** for her flower because her cheeks are always so rosy red in color. **Roses** grow in many colors and have many meanings of beauty, love, honor, and faith.

Alex and Alyssa grow their flowers side by side in the fairy garden. Sometimes they get in each other's way and argue. Their parents explain to them that being twins they are the same but different. They look alike and have the same birthday, but they are still their own individual selves. They must learn to work side by side and as twins to set a good example of teamwork for all the fairies in Blossom Land.

The second set of twins are both girls. December is known for miracles and indeed a miracle happened in Blossom Land when these two girls were born. An older fairy couple, Mr. and Mrs. Jolly, did not think they would ever have a child. All of their friends and relatives had at least one baby fairy, but year after year, they did not. Then, ten years ago on December 24, not only did they receive a baby fairy, they received two! Yes, another set of twins was born in Blossom Land! They are named Holly and Joy because they were born in December. In December people and fairies decorate their homes and yards with **holly and poinsettias.** It is the month that everyone celebrates great joy with Christmas, Hanukah, Kwanza, or whatever one believes in. It is a month of miracles. So in December, Holly Jolly and Joy Jolly were born. The **holly** plant is green in color and the **poinsettia** is red. As both of the girls, Holly and Joy, are identical twins, they both grow **holly and poinsettias** in their side by side gardens. They always dress the same, and both of them usually wear green and red. They have long brown hair that is braided, and they wear their flowers entwined in their hair.

Turquoise is the name of the jewel for December. It is a bluish green and is said to be a charm for love and success. Holly and Joy wanted to wear their jewel as a toe ring but it was too heavy on their little toes and would fall off whenever they wanted to fly, so they wear their stones around their necks with a chain made out of holly.

Now, with the help of the two sets of twins, the word would surely get out to the other classmates.

Sam was contacted by Alyssa. Sam was named after "Uncle Sam" because he was born on July 4. Of course he always dresses in red, white and blue and loves wearing stars and stripes. Sam's birthstone is the **red ruby.** It is similar in color to Snowdrop's January garnet. Sam is very proud of this **red ruby** and has it attached to the middle of a top hat that he likes to wear.

The July flower can be either a water **lily or a larkspur**. The **larkspur** can be pink, white, or mauve. Sam likes to plant both of these flowers because the twins, Alex and Alyssa, are his best friends and they are always willing to help him with his garden. It is the twin's way of practicing their team work and because Sam is their good friend. With the help of the twins, Sam was able to create a small pond on one side of the fairy garden. He created this pond because water lilies are those flat green pads that grow in water and frogs like to sit on. Around the pond is planted the three different colors of the larkspur. It is quite a beautiful sight! The larkspur represents love and Sam always says that he is in love with Alyssa. The pond is near the Magic Wishing Well so Sam was sure to be there for the meeting.

Alex sat with Doc for lunch and told him of the meeting. Doc had also been worried about graduating. Doc was born in August. His parents named him Doc because of the healing powers of his birthstone, the green **peridot** jewel. They are hoping that someday Doc will be the official "doctor of the fairies." He is very studious and always has his nose in a book. His parents have told him they want him to study hard to become a doctor but he must also work alongside all the other fairies to help create the beautiful fairy garden.

August has two flowers for the month. The **gladiolus** grows in a rainbow of colors and has a meaning of love. The **poppy** grows in red, white, and yellow. The **red poppy** is for happiness, the **white poppy** is for peace, and the **yellow poppy** is for wealth and success.

We know that fairies plant the **poppy** flower but an old tale says the **poppy** flower forms deep inside the earth and is brought up to the surface by volcanoes. Doc doesn't like to dress up too much but he always wears a **red poppy** on his shirt or jacket. He likes to carry a walking stick, or cane, and he has his green **peridot** jewel attached to the top of his cane where it shines brightly.

Doc confided in Alex that although his grades were good they were not as good as they should be to become a doctor. Doc said that Professor DoGood did not seem happy in school the past week and wondered what was troubling him.

Holly and Joy Jolly were able to contact the remaining classmates. They spoke with Angel, Peter, and Tommy. As you can tell, the fairies are named according to their birthstone, flower, or something that their birth month signifies.

Angel is a helpful fairy with long, curly, blond hair and blue eyes. Many of the boy fairies have a crush on her but she is determined to grow her flowers and help others to grow theirs. Angel says she will not bother with boyfriends until she is much older.

Angel's birthstone for her September birthday is a beautiful dark blue **sapphire**. Its meaning is to protect from envy and harm. It is also said to bring "heavenly blessings." The September flower is also blue. It is called the **morning glory** because the flower only blooms in the morning hours. By the time the sun sets each day, the flower is no longer in bloom, but don't worry as the next morning there will be new blooms until sunset. The **morning glory** grows as a vine, upward, almost as if it was growing up to the heavens. Do you think this is why Angel's parents gave her this name?

Angel uses a small vine of **morning glories** in a wreath around her hair. It looks pretty with the dark blue flowers against her blond curls. She wears her **sapphire** as a necklace to match her blue eyes.

The remaining two fairies in this year's graduation class are Peter and Tommy. These two boys are the busiest of the fairies. They both have double duty.

Peter was born in October. October brings a change of seasons. It begins the autumn of the year. You will usually see colors of yellow, brown, purple and orange decorating homes during this time. The flower for October is the **marigold. Marigolds** grow in white, gold, and yellow. The most popular color is bright orange, like the pumpkins that we carve for Halloween. **Marigolds** are edible and many fairies use them in salads.

October's jewel is an **opal or tourmaline** and means "precious stone." Both change color like the seasons do. The **opal** is usually milky white but can change in color even to black. The **tourmaline** comes in different colors. Both stones can change color with flashes of yellow, orange, green, red, or blue.

October 31 is Halloween. We dress up in costumes and go trick or treating. Fairies do not celebrate Halloween like we do. They cannot eat much candy because they are so small. If they gain too much weight, they would no longer be able to fly! We buy pumpkins and try to find the biggest ones we can to carve faces on them. Fairies grow little pumpkins and use paints and crayons to decorate them with flowers and designs. Once the fairies decorate their pumpkins, they give them to their parents to thank them for teaching them how to grow their gardens. On Halloween night, the fairies string up lights around the garden and the Magical Wishing Well. Their parents join them and they all sit in a circle and share stories about the good and not so good things that may have happened the past year. The fairies are usually excited because in a few months, they will find out if they graduate and receive magical powers at the wishing well! They try to see if their parents will give them a hint about the end of the year gift but their moms and dads will not budge. They tell all of their children that patience is a good virtue to have.

Peter grows the **marigolds** and he is the one responsible to grow the tiny fairy pumpkins. As you can probably guess, his favorite color is orange. He likes to dress in little denim blue jeans and usually wears an orange shirt with blue suspenders. His **opal** stone is woven into his little straw hat he wears over his short orange hair. Many of the other fairies have nicknamed him Peter Pumpkin but they all pitch in when they have time to help. They want to be sure they will all get their pumpkins.

Tommy was born in November. November is a time to reflect on everything we are thankful for. Humans celebrate Thanksgiving Day with a big turkey dinner. Fairies do not eat turkey. They spend the month thinking about the upcoming gift day in December and wondering if they have been thankful not only in November, but all through the year. It is the code of the fairies to be kind to one another all the time and to share their good fortunes with others, including humans. The flowers they have grown all year are given not only to their friends and family but to humans who live outside the village, especially when the fairies sense that the humans need a little extra care and love. Sometimes it is difficult for fairies to cover the entire area of the village, even though they can fly. This is especially the case during planting when they work hard and are tired by the end of the day. To help them out, Tommy started "Dragon Fly Delivery." Tommy has been thoughtful to not only his fellow fairies, but to the frogs in Sam's pond, and to all the insects in the garden. Because of this he developed a special friendship with the dragon flies. They agree to fly fairies, when needed, to deliver flowers and good wishes as sometimes with all the flowers, the load is too heavy for the fairies themselves to fly. You may think that Tommy was named after "Tommy Turkey" or "Tom Turkey," but remember that fairies do not eat turkey. Tommy got his name because when he was born he was only as big as his father's thumb, so this reminded his parents of "Tom Thumb." Now that Tommy is ten years old he has grown into a regular size fairy.

The long name for Tommy's birth month flower is the **chrysanthemum,** but everyone calls them **"mums"** for short. They grow in many colors. Tommy likes the gold color because it is like his November yellow-gold jewel **topaz.** The **topaz** has a special meaning of hope and energy. Tommy likes to dress in a yellow jumpsuit. He wears a little gold visor on his head and has made golden colored reins for the dragon flies in his "Dragon Fly Delivery" service. His **topaz** stone is worn on the top of his gold visor. You can see that Tommy has much hope and energy, like his stone, because he has made a successful garden of multiple colored mums and runs "Dragon Fly Delivery."

Chapter Four

Meeting of the Fairies

The plan was after school each fairy would go home, report to their parents about their school day, and then meet at the Magic Wishing Well before they started their daily garden work.

Once they were all gathered at the wishing well, Snowdrop and Freddy took the lead.

Snowdrop started the meeting, "We have called all of our classmates here today to try to help each other graduate. I want all of my friends to understand that I have to work very hard these last few months so I will not be able to play as much until all my work and studying is done. Please understand that I am not mad at any of you but I must do this to be sure I graduate."

All the other fairies talked at once saying they understood and they too must try extra hard.

Peter spoke up and said, "I think we are all good students but something is wrong with Professor DoGood. He doesn't seem happy. He isn't smiling much anymore. Maybe we have done something wrong."

All of a sudden they heard a rustling in the trees outside the garden. Everyone got quiet and turned toward the trees but did not see anything. The noise stopped.

Freddy spoke up, "Peter, I too have noticed that Professor DoGood does not seem the same. Do you think he could be ill or maybe disappointed in us?"

Lily chimed in, "My fellow fairies, we are all good students and we do our best. I don't think it is anything to do with us. Maybe Professor DoGood is ill. How can we find out and what can we do to make him feel better?"

The fairies then heard a soft chuckling in the trees. The birds were making a squawking sound, not their usual happy chirping. Someone was spying on the fairies! Freddy put his finger to his lips, then moved his fingers on his other hand up and down like a quacking duck as a sign to have the fairies keep talking while he quickly flew around the trees to see what the commotion was. He noticed there was a tall, thin fairy with a bag of gardening tools.

"Who are you and what are you doing in our garden?" Freddy asked with a firm voice.

"You silly children. You know nothing about what is happening in Blossom Land!"

"What are you talking about and who are you?" Freddy now shouted at this strange looking fairy.

The other fairies heard Freddy's raised voice and came around to see what was going on.

"Look at all of you in your colorful outfits trying to figure out what is wrong with your precious Professor DoGood. It is time for Professor DoGood to retire. It is time for Blossom Land to grow into a business and into the future, and I am the one to do that! My name is Mr. Snarley. I will be the new principal next year at Blossom Land Fairy School. You see, I am replacing Miss Cinnamon next year. She is getting married and moving away. I plan to take Blossom Land into the future. The fairies of Blossom Land spend too much time making "happy" and it doesn't get you anything or anywhere. You could live in cozy, modern condos and have cars like the humans, only much smaller of course. Think of the money you could make if you sold your flowers instead of just giving them away after you have done all that hard work in your gardens."

All the fairies fluttered about with their mouths open starring wide-eyed at each other. They could not believe what this Mr. Snarley was saying!

Snowdrop was the first to speak up, "How can you say such things? You are a fairy like us. Don't you live by the fairy code?"

"I come from Woodland Patch and we do not honor such a code. We don't have all your precious little flowers and jewels. We don't have dragon flies that help us with our work," Mr. Snarley replied gruffly.

Snowdrop sadly looked at Mr. Snarley, "I feel sorry for you. Maybe your village isn't as beautiful as ours but that isn't our fault. We don't need money or little cars. We receive our happiness by helping others."

Mr. Snarley laughed a mean laugh and said, "You won't have much choice now, will you? Next year I will be the new principal and all the future students will have to live by the new rules that I will write. If you have younger brothers and sisters they will need to understand through my teaching these new laws."

Freddy was so angry! He spoke up, "Just where do you intend to build all of these condos? There isn't enough room in Blossom Land!"

"Well, that is where you are wrong! Your gardens will be cut in half to make room for the condos."

"If you cut our gardens in half, how are you going to make enough money as the flowers you want to sell will be half as much?" Snowdrop asked.

Mr. Snarley smiled slyly as he stroked on his large black mustache, "We will charge a high price for the flowers. Humans and fairies will pay the price because Blossom Land is the only flower growing fairy land around."

Everyone was quiet as Mr. Snarley stood there with a wicked smile.

Finally, Freddy asked, "Does Professor DoGood know about this?"

"Of course he does, although, I must say he is not pleased with the idea. He is sworn to secrecy not to tell anyone until after graduation. I am sure it won't take any time at all to show the Professor that he is too old for his job. Enjoy these last few months tending to your gardens. The students next year will be working in the gardens part-time and selling the flowers part-time."

Mr. Snarley then just flew away.

"This is just awful!" Snowdrop cried. All the other fairies agreed.

"This must be why Professor DoGood seemed so unhappy," Freddy realized. "We have to do something about this. We can't lose Professor DoGood and we can't let that mean Mr. Snarley change Blossom Land. We must come up with a plan."

Chapter Five

A Plan?

"How can he be so mean?" Snowdrop wondered.

After Mr. Snarley flew off, all the fairies just sat in a circle and pouted.

"We have to do something, Freddy!" Snowdrop cried.

Freddy's voice was barely a whisper, "I was so concerned about myself graduating and now I am concerned for all of Blossom Land. Maybe we should speak with Professor DoGood."

"We can't do that," Angel replied. "Mr. Snarley said that Professor DoGood was sworn to secrecy."

The Jolly twins, Holly and Joy, were whispering to each other.

Snowdrop told them, "Please stop whispering. It is rude. If you have an idea to help, please share it with all of us."

Holly apologized, "I'm sorry, Snowdrop, I did not mean to whisper. My sister and I were just wondering about Mr. Snarley. We don't know him at all. Maybe we should try to find out more about him. Woodland Patch is somewhat far from here but I think we should do some detective work and figure out what this is all about and why Mr. Snarley is the way he is."

"Excellent idea," Tommy pitched in. "We can use the Dragon Fly Delivery Service to fly overhead so Mr. Snarley won't notice us."

"I don't know when we will have the time to do this as we are so busy tending to our gardens and studying," Freddy wondered out loud.

"Maybe if we all agree to stop fooling around in class and work hard on our school and garden work, we will have the time," Snowdrop suggested. "We should also look out for each other and if someone needs help and we are available, we should pitch in and help them. After all, this is for the future of our home, the future of Blossom Land and all the fairies that will graduate after us."

"OK," Peter agreed. "But I don't know how spying on Mr. Snarley will change anything. What difference will it make?"

"I guess we won't know until we find out more about Mr. Snarley, Freddy replied. "Let's not mention this to Professor DoGood or our parents, at least until we have a plan in place. Our parents will worry and insist we spend all our time studying and working. They will not want us to worry about grown-up problems."

Snowdrop suggested that the boys work out a schedule with Tommy and the Dragon Fly Delivery Service to take turns investigating Woodland Patch and Mr. Snarley. She had another plan for the girls. They would hop on one of Tommy's dragon flies and head over to have a long chat with Miss Cinnamon.

Everyone agreed. They would start immediately. It was a plan to try to make a plan.

Chapter Six

The Investigation

The next day Tommy made a schedule with the Dragon Fly Delivery Service to take turns investigating Woodland Patch and Mr. Snarley. First, he would have Sam and Doc fly over Woodland Patch to see how the village was setup and where the fairies lived. Alex and Peter would enter Woodland Patch and pretend they were moving there so they could question other fairies about their school and the teachers. Freddy, Patrick, and Tommy would deliver flowers to the hospital in Woodland Patch to find out more information about how Woodland Patch practiced their fairy code.

Sam and Doc flew high above Woodland Patch on the backs of dragon flies. From the aerial sight this high above the ground, it was clear that Woodland Patch was a drab, dark, wooded area. Both Sam and Doc noticed the area seemed to be damaged with broken limbs and branches scattered all about. They swooped down lower in hopes to locate some of the fairies to see what their homes were like. As they were descending, they noticed a definite smell. It was a heavy, smoky odor that filled their tiny nostrils. There must have been a recent fire in Woodland Patch! Sam and Doc pulled the gold colored reins of their dragon fly transportation so they slowed a bit. As they floated downward, they could see fairies peeking out from huge, charred tree limbs that had fallen onto the ground. They seemed to be afraid. Doc wanted to land and talk to the fairies. He wanted to know what happened and see if he could help them. It was decided Doc would stay and Sam would head back to Blossom Land. He needed to tell Alex and Peter to start their part of the investigation right away.

Doc landed softly on the scorched earth. Two fairies were whimpering under a split log.

"Please don't be afraid," Doc pleaded. "I only want to help you. My name is Doc and I am studying to be a doctor. Are you ill? What happened here?"

Slowly the two girl fairies came out from under the log. They held each other's hand. Their little clothes were torn and dirty. One was taller and older than the other one.

"Why are you here?" the older one asked.

Doc spoke softly to them so he would not frighten them away. "I came from Blossom Land. I heard there was another fairy land over here and wanted to check it out. Did you have a fire here? What happened?"

Tears rolled down the fairies' faces. The older one explained, "It happened on the fourth of July. Woodland Patch was once a beautiful forest with so many green pine trees. There were rows and rows of maple and oak trees. In autumn, their leaves would change color from green to yellow, gold, and orange. Now all we have are burnt, damaged trees. Our houses were destroyed in the fire and so were the birds' nests. It is so sad. Our young fairies can't go to school until we rebuild. Our principal is working hard to try to figure out what we are going to do."

"I am very sorry. How did the fire start?" Doc wanted to know.

"Well, we think it was from fireworks or a campfire that wasn't completely snuffed out by the humans. Woodland Patch used to be a peaceful place for people to visit on holidays. Families would come here for picnics and play games, barbecue food, and enjoy the clean, fresh air. Now it is destroyed."

"I am so sorry. Are the humans going to plant trees to try to rebuild the forest?" Doc asked.

"They want to replant the trees but it will take years for newly planted trees to grow into the forest it once was. The last we heard there was a builder who came and looked at the land. He wants to buy the land, uproot the remaining trees, and build houses for the humans. I don't know what we will do."

Doc shook his head and replied, "Please tell me your name. I want to talk with my friends in Blossom Land to see if there is anything we can do to help. I promise to come back and do whatever I can."

The older fairy put her arm around the younger one, "My name is Fern, and this is my daughter, Ivy. We need so much help. I don't think there is anything you can do but thank you for trying."

Doc said his goodbye with a promise to return. He hopped on the dragon fly and flew home to speak with the others.

Meanwhile, in another part of the forest, Alex and Peter had flown over in a hurry as instructed by Sam. They chatted with several of the younger, school-aged fairies in Woodland Patch. Everyone they spoke with gave the same story that their homeland was ruined by a fire and their school principal was working on getting them back into school. Most of the fairies were losing hope because they noticed a change in their principal, Mr. Snarley. He had been a good fairy who was in charge of the school. It was after the fire that he seemed to change. He had a large home in a gigantic tree in the middle of the forest. The home was big enough for his family. He lived with his wife, his four children, and his elderly parents. Mr. Snarley's father suffered from a bad back and used a cane to walk. The loss of Mr. Snarley's home put a burden on everyone, especially Mr. Snarley as he had to search to find a place big enough for his entire family. Besides this, all the parents from Woodland Patch told him how worried they were for their children who no longer had a school to go to. They expected him to find a solution.

Alex and Peter retuned to Blossom Land. They were deep in thought and now felt very differently toward Mr. Snarley.

Freddy, Patrick, and Tommy also felt differently after visiting Woodland Patch's hospital. The hospital seemed overcrowded. Many fairies being cared for had been hurt by burns and smoke inhalation from the fire. There were also human fire fighters in the hospital who were sad because they tried so hard to stop the fire before it destroyed their forest. The fire just moved too fast and was too powerful.

The next day, all the fairies met again at the Magic Wishing Well to discuss the findings of their investigations. They all agreed it had been good to "sleep" on what they found the previous day before meeting again. It gave all of them a chance to think about Woodland Patch and Mr. Snarley.

The fairies now understood why Mr. Snarley seemed so mean. He was doing what he thought was necessary to get his family into a better living area by moving from burned out Woodland Patch to the beautiful gardens of Blossom Land.   Mr. Snarley probably thought that by building "fairy condos" all the children from Woodland Patch could live and go to school in Blossom Land.

"What can we do to help them?" Freddy asked. "Blossom Land only has one teacher, Professor DoGood, and it sounds like he is leaving! We don't have room for the fairies of Woodland Patch."

Snowdrop spoke up to report what the girl fairies had looked into for the investigation. They had made a visit to Miss Cinnamon. They told her everything. Miss Cinnamon was very concerned and sorry that she would be leaving Blossom Land. She did not want any of these changes to take place. She was going to speak with her fiancé. She encouraged the girls to go back to their meeting and agree all the other graduating students should ask their parents what to do.

All the students felt bad. They didn't know how to solve this huge problem. They agreed to talk with their parents.   They also agreed to seek out Mr. Snarley and treat him with kindness as they were sorry he had lost his home. Maybe another solution could be found.

Chapter Seven

Hope

The months of October and November seemed to drag on with the students working harder than ever tending to their gardens. They were worried that it would be the last year their gardens would be so lovely. They wanted this year's gardens to be extra special.

It was so quiet in Blossom Land. Freddy and Patrick no longer felt like joking with others. Snowdrop and her girlfriends didn't have to worry about spending less time playing because all they wanted to do was work their gardens for the last time.

Throughout these next months, Mr. Snarley made several appearances in the gardens while the students worked. It was difficult to accept, but the Blossom Land fairies tried their best to put aside their unfortunate fate and show only kindness to the wounded Mr. Snarley. Snowdrop would gather up many of the edible flowers and make a tasty salad for Mr. Snarley.

The first few times he responded with, "Why are you doing this? Don't think that you can try to win me over with feeding me. It will change nothing."

"We have accepted that our gardens will be smaller and that you will build your condos. We are sad but there is nothing we can do about it. We are thankful for all that we have had and we want to share it with you and Woodland Patch. Please just accept our friendship," Snowdrop begged.

"Humph!" Mr. Snarley grunted as he took the salad and left.

When the students told their parents as Miss Cinnamon had encouraged, they were surprised that they already knew! The parents did not want their children to worry about such matters. Now it was too late. All the parents encouraged the students not to change anything for now, but that was easier said than done. Parents were attending regular meetings with school and village officials to try to find a solution for the problem. It would take months to figure out, maybe even a year because they needed to find another teacher for all the extra students. The most important thing was to be sure the fairy families of Woodland Patch needed to be helped with their homes and schooling.

The Blossom Land fairies kept their promise to Fern and Ivy of Woodland Patch. They all took turns visiting the damaged forest and bringing families and hospitals small bouquets of flowers. They were sorry there was not much they were able to do but they wanted Woodland Patch to know they would happily accept them in their land. They were happy to have new friends. The concerns were that there would not be enough teachers and they were sad about cutting out half of the fairy gardens to build condos.

Peter's pumpkin patch thrived with small but perfectly round pumpkins. Peter asked the other fairies what they thought of giving the pumpkins to the Woodland Patch fairies this year instead of their parents. They thought it was a great idea. Their parents were happy and wanted to help too. Everyone pitched in and painted the pumpkins with flowers, stars, and hearts. They made a special one for Mr. Snarley and wrote, "Welcome to Blossom Land" on his. Then Tommy set up his Dragon Fly Delivery Service to make several trips to deliver the tiny pumpkins. The Woodland fairies were so happy. They smiled from ear to ear. They danced around the little decorated pumpkins and giggled with joy! It was such a happy sight to see. Next, Peter invited all the Woodland fairies to join them on Halloween. They would sit in Blossom Land's garden around the Magical Wishing Well and tell stories. The fairy garden would have bright lights strung up and it would be a good time to get to know everyone. Peter would help by supplying transportation with his Dragon Fly Delivery Service.

When Mr. Snarley received his "Welcome to Blossom Land" decorated pumpkin he didn't know what to say. He just accepted it, mumbled a "thank you," and hung his head down as he walked away.

Work continued through the autumn season. Every day the fairies would try to honor the fairy code "Spread beauty, hope, and friendship by working hard and helping others." Hadn't they been doing that forever? It was the season of Thanksgiving and the fairies all knew they had been truly blessed all of their lives. It was still difficult to know their land would soon change.

On Thanksgiving Day, Miss Cinnamon and her fiancé, Mr. Frost, surprised the fairies with a visit to the fairy garden. Mr. Frost wanted to introduce himself and explain to the fairies that he was sorry Miss Cinnamon would be leaving their school. He encouraged them to have hope. Together, they were all searching for ways to help both Woodland Patch and Blossom Land.

Then, another surprise happened! Mr. Snarley came to the garden and spoke. You could tell he was nervous as he hesitated and did not look the fairies in the eye. After a while, he took a deep breath and spoke.

"To the entire Blossom Land village, I want to thank you for all the kindness you have shown to Woodland Patch and especially to me. I did not make this easy for you. I tried to pretend that I was a bully so that I could protect and help Woodland Patch. After the humans destroyed our forest, I wanted the fairies of Woodland Patch to be happy again. I wanted to give them hope. This was not the way to give hope. You have all shown me that hope comes from the heart and is shown by your kindness, care, and love. It is too late to change what I have started as the condos for Blossom Land have been approved. The building of the condos will start right after your graduation ceremony."

A big sigh came from the audience of the fairies.

Mr. Snarley continued, "I want to be able to live like you. If I can only be half as kind and understanding as you, I will feel blessed. That is my hope."

Stillness hovered over the fairy garden. Each fairy had their own thoughts.

Miss Cinnamon spoke again, "Fellow students and parents, please remember that we are still working on final details for next year. Please don't worry. You must have hope that we are working to make a better place for all of Blossom Land and Woodland Patch. We will announce final plans on graduation day. Meanwhile, let us be thankful for all we have now and remember, December is the time for miracles."

Chapter Eight

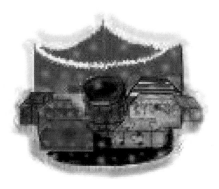

Miracles Do Happen

It was mid-December and excitement filled the air! Only a few of the fairies were a little worried. They did not want to go to the celebration and be embarrassed if they would not be receiving their gift. Most of all they were still worried about the final news for Blossom Land.

Freddy and Patrick were both wondering how they could start selling flowers for money after they had received so much joy out of giving them as gifts.

The December twins, Holly and Joy Jolly, were busy decorating all of Blossom Land with their poinsettias and holly. Tommy arranged for transportation with Dragon Fly Delivery to bring the red and green decorations to Woodland Patch. The land was still as it was after the fire and the fairies wanted to cheer it up for this season of miracles.

The fairy garden in Blossom Land was surprisingly quiet for the next few weeks. Each fairy had their own thoughts and dreams and wondered how life after December 31 would change.

The day of revelation had come! Every fairy family got up early in the morning to do all of their chores. This would leave them plenty of time to get extra spruced up for the big night. Their jewels would be highly polished and worn along with the most colorful flowers in their garden. The girls spent extra time decorating their hair with flowers and glitter. Some even painted flowers on their faces as they had done on May Day.

Just before sunset, the crowd arrived. Sparkling lights were hung around the garden and the wishing well. Dragon flies and lightening bugs created not only a buzz but an extra flicker of light. Around the Magic Wishing Well was a circle of colorful little treasure chests. Each treasure chest had a name tag and a big bow on it. The bow was the color of each one's birthday month jewel. The graduating fairies were instructed by their teacher, Professor DoGood, to sit on the ground next to their parents by the treasure chest with their name. Each fairy would be called up one at a time to be told if they passed the fairy code and would graduate. They would have to wait until every fairy was told their fate. Only then, could they open their tiny treasure chests and their magical gifts would be revealed.

The first one to be called was Snowdrop. She stood by the professor with her parents as he spoke.

"Snowdrop, you have proven to be a true friend to everyone, like the meaning of your carnation flower. You have learned to kindly tell your friends that your work comes first but you still want to visit with them after your work in the garden is done. Your garden was beautiful this year as it was well seeded, like the meaning of your jewel, the garnet. Congratulations, you have passed the test and will be awarded with a magical power."

The circle of fairies yelled out their congratulations and flapped their wings in celebration.

Next was Freddy the Flirt. After Freddy stood up, Professor DoGood said, "I want to do something different. I call up Patrick at the same time."

Patrick got so nervous he just knew that this was it! He and Freddy would not be given any power because of their joking around. Patrick gulped and stood silent next to Freddy, with his heart beating fast.

Professor DoGood began his speech, "Freddy, we all know that you are nicknamed Freddy the Flirt. You have a weakness for the beautiful fairies and all of our fairies are beautiful. You also share a gift of gab with your friend Patrick. You spend much time telling silly jokes."

Freddy and Patrick looked at each other with fear in their eyes.

"However," Professor DoGood continued, "neither one of you are mean to anyone. Your jokes are cute and are about silly things, not about people or other fairies. Freddy, you flirt and make the girls blush but you believe in true love. Someday you will find true love with one girl and you will no longer be known as "the flirt." You both have been so worried about the fate of Blossom Land. Instead of pouting, you two helped to make the Woodland fairies, especially Mr. Snarley, feel welcome. You listened to each other and supported each other as true friends should do. Therefore, you have shown a gift of true friendship and kindness, although sometimes silly. Congratulations to both of you!"

Next, Sweet Pea and Lily were recognized for their kindness and good gardening skills. They were commended for all of their hard work in preparing for the annual May Day celebration.

"I want to save the twins until last," Professor DoGood said. "We have two sets of twins this year and we will discuss them last."

"Oh my goodness," Holly and Joy said at the same time. They looked over at Alex and Alyssa with wonder and some worry in their eyes.

"It will be OK," Alyssa mouthed to Holly and Joy. Alex took Alyssa's hand and held it to comfort her.

"I now call up, Sam." Professor DoGood continued.

As Sam approached in his patriotic red, white, and blue with the ruby jewel in the center of his top hat, you couldn't help but notice how proud Sam was of his beloved Blossom Land and all the hard work that everyone put into their gardens. He winked at Alyssa as he passed by her.

Professor DoGood greeted Sam with a salute and praised him for doing double duty by planting Larkspurs and creating the lovely pond with water lilies. Sam had created a home for friends, the frogs and dragon flies. There was no doubt of Sam's passion and respect for all.

Doc was honored next for his caring of others and his desire to study medicine.

Angel was acknowledged for her kindness to others and her morning glories.

Peter and Tommy received special thanks for their gift of giving to the community. Peter for the little pumpkins and Tommy for the very useful "Dragon Fly Delivery."

"Last, but not least," Professor DoGood said, "please come forward, Alex and Alyssa, and Holly and Joy."

Both sets of twins were nervous as they approached the professor with their parents. Their parents had whispered to them not to worry. They were winners in their parents eyes no matter what happened.

Professor DoGood began, "All of us gathered here tonight knowing what hard work it is to tend to our gardens, go to fairy school, and practice the fairy code. We all have good days and bad days. Sometimes we get along just great but sometimes we argue. No one person or fairy is perfect but we need to live, work and play together. Before you we see two sets of twins. They are so much alike yet they are different. They are unique individuals like you and me. Can you imagine how difficult it is for two people who look alike and talk alike to work and play side by side without ever having a problem? I would say it is next to impossible. The secret of living this way is to be forgiving and understanding. If you have a quarrel, after you have cooled off, be sure to say, "I'm sorry." Don't hold grudges. I know that Alex and Alyssa don't always get along with each other but they never stay mad for long. They are both helpful and caring. Alex grows beautiful honeysuckle flowers

48

to feed the hummingbirds and Alyssa shows good teamwork helping with the pond. Now look at Holly and Joy Jolly! They are truly identical twins. We can hardly tell them apart. I know that they will both have success and love in their lives because they help everyone. They decorate Blossom Land with holly and poinsettia's during holidays but they don't expect anything in return. They are truly giving people. Congratulations to all of you as you will all receive your special gift."

Hoots and hollers filled the air! The fairies all held hands and danced around in a big circle.

After a while, Professor DoGood asked all to take their places next to their treasure boxes. Professor DoGood stood in front of the Magical Wishing Well to give the final instructions.

"Before you open your treasure chests, I must explain that the gift inside your treasure chest is a gift but that isn't all it is."

The fairies had looks of confusion on their faces.

Professor DoGood said, "Please open your treasure boxes to see what is inside but then remain seated."

Each fairy carefully removed the colorful bow and opened the gold latch that secured their treasure chest. Inside each treasure chest was a beautiful jewel! It was the same color as the stone they received for their birthday month. These stones were much bigger and much brighter than any stone they had. There were many 'Oohs' and 'Aahs' at the glare from these brilliant stones.

Sweet Pea asked, "How are we to wear such a large jewel."

Holly and Joy added, "Yes how will we do that as we tried to wear toe rings with our smaller jewel and they were even too big."

"Hush everyone," Professor DoGood said. "Listen to me carefully. You have been given this larger jewel but it is not the true gift you will receive. Each one of you will take a turn and put your jewel in the wishing well bucket. You will then crank the handle to lower the bucket. You will wait for a bell to ring, and then your true gift will be revealed. You must trust me that what the Magical Wishing Well gives you in return will be your true gift and magical power."

One by one, the fairies took turns. Snowdrop was first. She put her brilliant garnet in the bucket and slowly lowered it into the wishing well. It was so dark in the wishing well she could not see the bottom. After a few minutes, everyone heard a bell ring and the professor said, "It is time for you to pull up your magical gift."

Snowdrop turned the handle of the wishing well. The bucket seemed much heavier than when she put her stone in. As the bucket came up a glorious glow of sparkling red glitter filled the bucket.

"What is it, Professor? And what is it for?" Snowdrop shouted.

"Your jewel has been turned into magical fairy dust. This fairy dust has the magical power that was given to you in your flowers and jewels. Snowdrop, you have the special gift of planting a bountiful garden and you were blessed by the gifts of affection, love, and true friendship that your parents presented to you. Every one of you will receive the magical fairy dust in exchange for the jewel in your treasure chest. You will find a silk bag attached inside the top

50

of your chest. You are to keep the fairy dust inside your treasure chest but always carry with you the silk bag filled with some of the magical fairy dust. You will use the fairy dust to spread to those who do not have what you have, or to help others when they need a friend. They are not to know who blessed them or why. Keep your treasure chests safe and they will always be magically full. They will never empty as long as you continue to live by the fairy code and share your gifts with others. You see, the true gift is not that you have received a bigger jewel, it is that you will always share the gifts you were given."

The evening continued with the bell ringing and the magical changing of jewels into fairy dust. The colors were brilliant with everyone's different colors and once all the fairies exchanged their jewels a huge rainbow of many colors glowed over the entire length of the fairy garden. Everyone was happy and excited to spread their gifts to those less fortunate than themselves.

"What about next year?" Sam asked. "Maybe we could have given our jewels to you and Mr. Snarley. You could have gotten enough money for them and we could have saved Blossom Land and Woodland Patch.

"That is what I love so much about our students," Professor DoGood responded.

"You were given a wonderful gift and yet you are still concerned about our future. This is the main reason I have decided to stay as a teacher at Blossom Land."

The fairies shouted with glee.

"Let me continue," Professor DoGood said. "There will still be changes. As you know, Mr. Snarley did tell you at Thanksgiving that Woodland Patch has been sold to build homes for the humans. We have been working hard with everyone to make the best changes for Blossom Land. Woodland Patch received enough money from the builder to be able to help us. They want to return our kindness. The builder who will be building the homes for the humans in Woodland Patch will first come to Blossom Land and build little homes for fairies."

Sighs were heard and silence filled the air.

Professor DoGood smiled and said, "You will be happy to know that the homes will be built but you will not have to reduce the size of any of your fairy gardens."

"How is that possible?" several fairies yelled out.

"Remember you all kept hope and continued working for what was best for everyone. The builder has come up with a plan for little fairy homes that will hang from the branches of our trees! We have seen drawings of his plans and they look like little cottages that will be hidden by the leaves on the trees. There will be room for everyone! Best of all, we will not have to sell our flowers for money as Woodland Patch made enough money from selling the land to pay for the cottages. Now, Mr. Snarley wants to say a few words."

Mr. Snarley stood up with a smile on his face. "You have all given me the greatest gift I could have received. You showed me how kindness and beauty are more important than money. Your friendship is worth more than anything money could buy. I will have a comfortable home now for my family and my aging father. With school starting next month, it will be tight in space with the addition of the students from Woodland Patch. This will change. We will be adding on to the school. Also, as the new principal of Blossom Land, I no longer want any of you to wear uniforms. I want to see the beauty of your hard work in the flowers and colors you wear. I am happy Professor DoGood has agreed to stay but it will be too much work for him with so many more students. I have hired one more teacher. Please welcome Mr. Frost."

"Oh my goodness," Holly and Joy squealed with delight at the same time. "We thought you and Miss Cinnamon were getting married and moving to another town."

Miss Cinnamon came out and held Mr. Frost's hand. She smiled at him, turned to face all the students and explained, "When the girls from this graduation class came to visit me about what was happening with Woodland Patch, my heart went out to them. I love Blossom Land and wanted to do whatever I could to help. Mr. Frost saw how sad I was and he wanted to help. Once the land was sold with more than enough money available to Blossom Land, Mr. Frost suggested he would ask Mr. Snarley for a teaching job so when we get married we could live here. Both Mr. Snarley and Professor DoGood agreed, and I will be available as a substitute teacher so when Professor DoGood wants to take some time off, I will fill in."

After months of worrying, everyone was so happy. This was the best way things could have turned out.

"One more announcement," Miss Cinnamon added. "Mr. Frost and I plan to be married this coming spring when your fairy gardens are in full bloom. We want to have the wedding in the fairy garden with all of you invited. I want you to help with the decorations and my dress. It will be another wonderful celebration."

That night, as Holly and Joy Jolly were getting ready for bed, they asked their parents to tuck them in. They wanted to talk about what a big day it had been.

"Do miracles always happen in December?" Holly asked. "That is the month we were born."

Then Joy said, "How can it be that our treasure chest will never be empty? How will it get refilled once we start spreading our fairy dust?"

"Let's answer one question at a time," Mr. Jolly replied. "Yes, you two were born in December and that was a miracle. Every life is a miracle so everyone has it inside them to do miracles by sharing the gifts they were born with."

Mrs. Jolly said, "In answer to your second question, there is an old saying that it is better to give than to receive. This year you have found out that by giving of yourself you have received a great gift. You gave friendship, beauty, and hope to Woodland Patch when they lost everything. In return you received those gifts back. Look at all the new friends you will have. Your treasure chest will always be full as long as you give of yourselves to help others."

The girls kissed their mom and dad goodnight. They closed their eyes with smiles on their faces. They dreamt of the wonder of the past year and knew that each day was indeed a miracle.

Month	Flower	Meaning	Jewel	Meaning
January		**Carnation** - affection, love, true friendship, seeding		**Garnet** – eternal friendship, trust
February		**Violet** – wisdom, hope, faith		**Amethyst** – myths, legends, quick witted
March		**Daffodil** - respect, rebirth		**Aquamarine** – water, sea, to calm and protect
April		**Sweet Pea** – love and gratitude		**Diamond** – Love
May		**Lily of the Valley** - happiness, sweetness		**Emerald** – good fortune, youth, rebirth

Month	Flower	Meaning	Jewel	Meaning
June		**Honeysuckle** - love, appreciation		**Alexandrite (Moonstone)** – good health, love, beauty, faith
		Rose – love, appreciation		**Pearl** – good health, love, beauty, faith
July		**Larkspur** – sweetness		**Ruby** – courage, devotion
		Lily – Sweetness		
August		**Poppy**- remembrance, wealth, success		**Peridot** – magical healing powers
		Gladiolus- remembrance, wealth, success		

Month	Flower	Meaning	Jewel	Meaning
September		**Morning Glory** - magic, love, patience		**Sapphire** – protect from harm, heavenly blessings
October		**Marigold** – grace		**Opal** – precious stone
November		**Chrysanthemum** - compassion, friendship, secret love		**Topaz** – hope, energy
December		**Holly** – faith, sweetness		**Turquoise** – love, success
		Poinsettia – faith, sweetness		